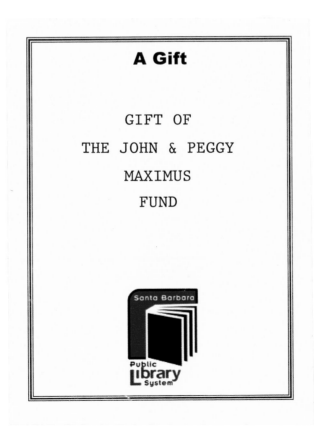

W

The Child's World

Published in the United States of America by The Child's World®
1980 Lookout Drive • Mankato, MN 56003-1705
800-599-READ • www.childsworld.com

ACKNOWLEDGMENTS
The Child's World®: Mary Berendes, Publishing Director
The Design Lab: Kathleen Petelinsek, Design and Page Production
Literacy Consultants: Cecilia Minden, PhD, and Joanne Meier, PhD

LIBRARY OF CONGRESS
CATALOGING-IN-PUBLICATION DATA
Moncure, Jane Belk.
  My "w" sound box / by Jane Belk Moncure;
illustrated by Rebecca Thornburgh.
    p. cm. — (Sound box books)
  Summary: "Little w has an adventure with items beginning with
her letter's sound, such as woodpeckers, a wolf, a wishing wand,
some watermelons, and wonderfully wiggly worms."–Provided by
publisher.
  ISBN 978-1-60253-163-5 (library bound : alk. paper)
  [1. Alphabet.] I. Thornburgh, Rebecca McKillip, ill. II. Title.
III. Series.
  PZ7.M739Myw 2009
  [E]—dc22   2008033179

A NOTE TO PARENTS AND EDUCATORS:

Magic moon machines and five fat frogs are just a few of the fun things you can share with children by reading books with them. Reading aloud helps children in so many ways! It introduces them to new words, motivates them to develop their own reading skills, and expands their attention span and listening abilities. So it's important to find time each day to share a book or two . . . or three!

As you read with young children, you can help develop their understanding of how print works by talking about the parts of the book—the cover, the title, the illustrations, and the words that tell the story. As you read, use your finger to point to each word, modeling a gentle sweep from left to right.

Simple word games help develop important prereading skills, including an understanding of rhyme and alliteration (when words share the same beginning sound, such as "six" and "sand"). Try playing with words from a book you've just shared: "What other words start with the same sound as moon?" "Cat and hat, do those words rhyme?" The possibilities are endless—and so are the rewards!

My "w" Sound Box®

(The "wh" sound is included in this book.)

WRITTEN BY JANE BELK MONCURE

ILLUSTRATED BY REBECCA THORNBURGH

Little 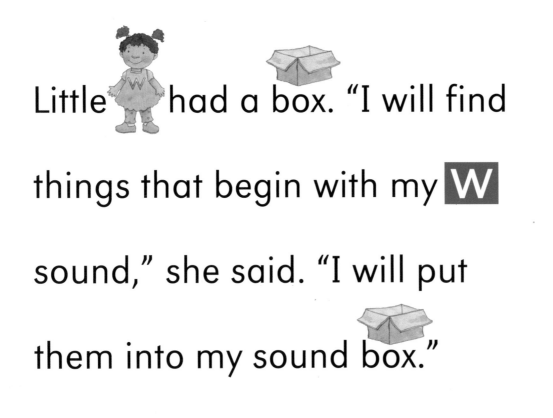 had a box. "I will find

things that begin with my **W**

sound," she said. "I will put

them into my sound box."

Little 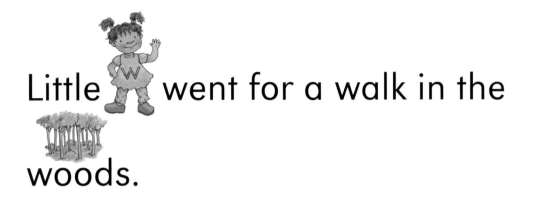 went for a walk in the woods.

She found woodpeckers and a  woodchuck. Did she put them into her box? She did.

Little  looked under some wood chips. She found lots of wiggly worms.

"In you go," she said.

Little  walked to a well in the woods. She saw some water in the well.

"This may be a wishing well,"

she said. She looked all around

the well.

Guess what she found? A wand!

Little  waved the wand and

made a wish. "I wish I could

find more things for my box,"

she said.

Just then, a weasel wiggled into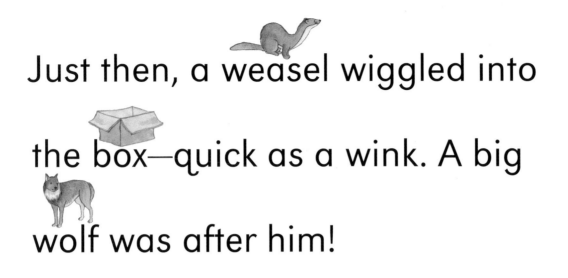

the box—quick as a wink. A big

wolf was after him!

Little 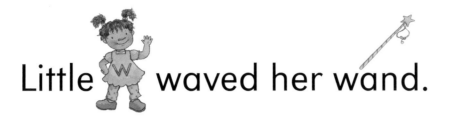 waved her wand.

"I wish you would be a good

wolf," she said.

She put the wolf into her box

with the weasel, the woodpecker,

the wiggly worms, and the

woodchuck. Now the box was full.

Little 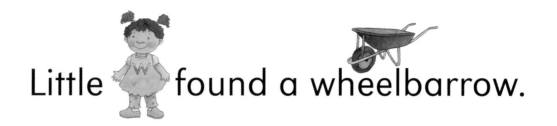 found a wheelbarrow.

"Whee!" she said. "This is just

what I need."

She wheeled the wheelbarrow.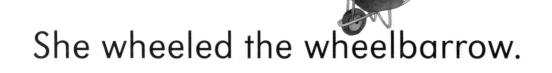

Away they went, along a winding

road to the water. "Let's wade in

the water," she said.

But the wolf, weasel, woodpecker, wiggly worms, and woodchuck did not want to wade. They watched.

"Wow!" said a walrus. "You look

wacky to me. You have funny feet."

"You look wacky to me," said

Little  . "You have funny

whiskers."

Little  put the walrus into the box. The walrus winked at the wolf.

Little  went back to the water.

The wind blew the waves up and

down.

Then she saw a big whale. The

whale whistled. "I wish I could

put the whale in my box, but it is

too big," she said.

Little  waved her wand and found a big wagon. It was big enough for a whale!

She put everything into the wagon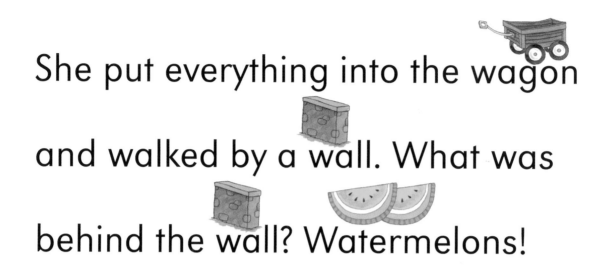

and walked by a wall. What was

behind the wall? Watermelons!

"Whoopee!" whooped the woodpeckers when they saw the watermelons.

"Let's have a watermelon party,"

said Little .

And they did.

Little 's Word List

wagon	weasel	wolf
wall	well	wood chips
walrus	whale	woodchuck
wand	wheelbarrow	woodpecker
water	whiskers	woods
watermelon	wind	worm
wave	wishing well	

Other Words with Little

waffle

wallet

walnut

wasp

watch

waterfall

web

wheel

wheelchair

whistle

wig

windmill

window

wing

woman

More to Do!

Little  found many **W** things on her walk. Here's a silly rhyming **W** word game you can play on your own or with friends.

Directions:

Repeat the first three lines of the verse below. For the last line, fill in your own **W** word and silly ending to the sentence.

Rhyming:

We went walking. Wild, wild walking.
We walked high, we walked low.
We walked some more, and what do you know?
We saw waffles! Wiggly wiggly waffles. Yum!

We went walking. Wild, wild walking.
We walked high, we walked low.
We walked some more, and what do you know?
We saw wheels! Big round wheels. Wheeeeee!

Your Turn!

Here are some 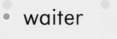 words to help you get started:

- waiter
- wax
- weeds
- wheat
- wire
- wrappers
- wren

About the Author

Best-selling author Jane Belk Moncure has written over 300 books throughout her teaching and writing career. After earning a Master's degree in Early Childhood Education from Columbia University, she became one of the pioneers in that field. In 1956, she helped form the Virginia Association for Early Childhood Education, which established the first statewide standards for teachers of young children.

Inspired by her work in the classroom, Mrs. Moncure's books have become standards in primary education, and her name is recognized across the country. Her success is reflected not only in her books' popularity with parents, children, and educators, but also by numerous awards, including the 1984 C. S. Lewis Gold Medal Award.

About the Illustrator

Rebecca Thornburgh lives in a pleasantly spooky old house in Philadelphia. If she's not at her drawing table, she's reading—or singing with her band, called Reckless Amateurs. Rebecca has one husband, two daughters, and two silly dogs.